J O I N T H E T E A M !

Do you watch GHOSTWRITER on PBS? Then you know that when you read and write to solve a mystery or unravel a puzzle, you're using the same smarts and skills the Ghostwriter team uses.

We hope you'll join the team and read along to help solve the mysterious and puzzling goings-on in these GHOSTWRITER books!

RALLY!

a Year's Supply of Fun

by SUSAN LURIE

illustrated by Nelle Davis

A CHILDREN'S TELEVISION WORKSHOP BOOK

BANTAM BOOKS
NEW YORK • TORONTO • LONDON • SYDNEY • AUCKLAND

Rally! A Year's Supply of Fun

A Bantam Book / December 1993

Ghostwriter, **Ghost**writer and ● are
trademarks of Children's Television Workshop.
All rights reserved. Used under authorization.

Cover design by Susan Herr
Cover photography by Walt Chrynwski
Original interior illustrations by Nelle Davis
Portraits by Phil Franke
Art direction by Marva Martin

ISBN 0-553-48092-8

Published simultaneously in the United States and Canada

Bantam Books are published by Bantam Books, a division of Bantam Doubleday Dell Publishing Group, Inc. Its trademark, consisting
of the words "Bantam Books" and the portrayal of a rooster, is
Registered in U.S. Patent and Trademark Office and in other countries. Marca Registrada. Bantam Books, 1540 Broadway, New York,
New York 10036.

PRINTED IN THE UNITED STATES OF AMERICA

cwo   0 9 8 7 6 5 4 3 2 1

Hey, what's up? Are you looking for something new and different to do? Well, the Ghostwriter team can help. Is it January? Celebrate Kazoo Day with your own kazoo band. March? Make your own movie, in honor of the Oscar Awards. (We'll show you how to do it without a camera!) September? Give your grandparents a family tree for Grandparents' Day. November? Of course—it's Sandwich Month. Check out our favorite recipes, or come up with your own.

The thing is, almost every day of the year is special for *someone*. People celebrate the weirdest things! Like Pet Owners Independence Day. Or Aardvark Week. Or—check this out—the Decade of the Brain! Weird, huh?

We here on the Ghostwriter team decided to round up our favorite events and tell you how *you* can celebrate them. Some are weird, and some are not so weird. But all in all, they add up to a year's worth of fun. So . . . have fun!

Signed,

Jamal *Lenni*

Alex *Gaby*

Tina *Rob*

THERE'S A FUTURE IN FORTUNE COOKIES!

The Chinese New Year is a cool (and we don't mean cold!) winter holiday. The exact date changes every year, but it falls on the new moon, usually in late January or early February. This year the Ghostwriter team went to Chinatown to see the parade and the dragon dance. And Lenni's dad Max made fortune cookies! The team pitched in and made up cool fortunes to go inside.

Follow the recipe on page 5 to make your own fortune cookies. And while you're at it, make up your own fortunes to go inside! Write them in the spaces on pages 3–4, and then cut them out. The team filled in a few to get you started.

Did you know that fortune cookies aren't really an ancient Chinese recipe at all? They were invented right here in the United States by Chinese people who came here in the 1800s.

Gaby

The Vietnamese New Year, called Tet, is celebrated at the same time as the Chinese New Year. My family celebrates Tet with a big Vietnamese feast. Yum!

Tina

Your hair will turn green tomorrow.

If you can find the problem with with this fortune, your wish will come true.

You will become very, very annoyed...
(Please turn over.)

You will become very, very
annoyed...
(Please turn over.)

Stuff you need:

¾ cup unbeaten egg whites
(you'll need about five or six
eggs, plus a grown-up to help
you separate them)
1⅔ cups sugar
¼ teaspoon salt

1 cup melted butter
1 cup all-purpose flour
¾ cup finely chopped almonds
½ teaspoon vanilla
Scissors
Pen or pencil

What you do:

1. Follow the lines and cut the fortunes pages into strips. Write a fortune on each strip. Then use your own paper to write more fortunes—you'll need about 60.

2. Preheat the oven to 350°. In a mixing bowl, mix the egg whites, sugar, and salt. Make sure they're well mixed.

3. Stir in the rest of the ingredients. Beat well.

4. Drop teaspoonfuls of dough onto an ungreased baking sheet. Make sure there's plenty of space between the blobs of dough. They'll spread out a lot!

5. Bake about ten minutes, or until cookies are flat and their edges are golden brown.

6. Get your grown-up to help you curl each cookie over a wooden spoon handle, like this:

Be careful not to burn your fingers.

7. After you curl the cookies, slide one fortune into the center of each. The ends of the fortune should stick out slightly. Pinch the ends of the cookies closed while they're still warm.

8. Give the cookies out to your friends!

Did you know that January 28 is National Kazoo Day? Word—it's true! When the Ghostwriter team read about Kazoo Day, they decided it was *so* weird they had to celebrate it. Lenni made up a rap. The rest of the team played along with her—on kazoos that Jamal made!

Jamal's paper kazoo works differently from the metal kind. He calls it a Ka-buzz. Here's how to make it.

Stuff you need:
- scissors
- tape
- pencil or pen
- sheet of notebook or copier paper

What you do:

First, cut your sheet of paper into a square. Then:

1. Starting at one corner, roll the paper into a tube. Use your pen or pencil as a guide as in step 1 of the drawing.

2. When the tube is rolled, tape it in the middle to keep it from unrolling. Remove the pen or pencil.

3. Carefully cut a notch at one end of the tube (see dotted line in drawing). It should now have a flap at that end, shaped like an arrowhead. Fold the flap to cover that end of the tube.

4. Put the uncut end of the tube in your mouth. Inhale! The flap should make a buzzing noise, like a duck's quack. It takes practice to get a good sound, so keep trying!

BEST FRIENDS

February 14 is Valentine's Day—a good time to do something fun with your best friend. How about a friendship quiz? Jamal and Lenni know practically everything about each other. How much do you know about *your* best friend?

What you do:

1. Answer the quiz questions below and on the next page as you think your friend would.

2. Call your best friend and check your answers. How many did you get right?

3. Figure out your score. For each question you got right, give yourself the number of points listed at the top of that section.

4. Look up your rating on the chart below. How well *do* you know your best friend?

35 . . . . You must be a mind reader!

27–34 . . . . Congrats! You know your best friend very well.

21–26 . . . . Not bad—but there's room for improvement.

16–20 . . . . We-e-ellll . . .

0–15 . . . . Yikes! You and what's-its-name need to spend some quality time!

1 point each

    1. Favorite color:

    2. Favorite TV show:

    3. Favorite movie:

    4. Favorite book:

5. Favorite kind of music:

6. Favorite sport:

2 points each

If your friend had to choose one thing to do in each pair, which would it be?

1. a) See a movie □
   b) Read a book □
2. a) Talk on the phone □
   b) Write a letter □
3. a) Eat a hamburger □
   b) Eat an apple □
4. a) Ride a bike □
   b) Watch TV □

3 points each

1. If your friend could travel to any country in the world, where would he/she go?

2. If your friend had to eat the same thing for lunch every day, what would that be?

3. If your friend had a million dollars, what would he/she buy first?

4. If your friend could meet any sports star, who would it be?

5. If your friend could meet any movie star, who would it be?

6. If tomorrow were your friend's birthday, what birthday gift would he/she want the most in the world?

7. If your friend could change one thing about himself/herself, what would he/she want to change?

The third Monday in February is Presidents' Day. It's a holiday to honor all the Presidents of the United States. Alex especially likes Presidents' Day—he's hoping that one day it'll honor President Alejandro Fernandez!

In the meantime, though, Alex is celebrating Presidents' Day by writing a letter to the White House. There are a few things he wants to tell the President. Alex has some ideas on how the job should be done. . . .

Do you have something you'd like to say to the President? How do you think the country's doing? What do you think the President is doing well? What do you think he could do better? What things are you worried about? Use the next page to write and get it off your chest!

When your letter is done, carefully cut the page along the dotted line. Then fold it over along the solid line. Seal it with a small piece of tape, put a stamp on it, and drop it in the nearest mailbox!

Hey! Don't forget to write your return address on the black lines on back of your letter. That way the post office can send it back to you if anything goes wrong.

Alex

THE PRESIDENT OF THE UNITED STATES
THE WHITE HOUSE
1600 PENNSYLVANIA AVENUE
WASHINGTON, D.C. 20501

DEAR MR. PRESIDENT:

SINCERELY,

_____

(YOUR NAME)

THE PRESIDENT OF THE UNITED STATES
THE WHITE HOUSE
1600 PENNSYLVANIA AVENUE
WASHINGTON, D.C. 20501

FOLD

MOVIE MAGIC

March is Academy Awards month. Tina loves to watch the Oscars on TV. She plans to be a filmmaker, and she hopes to win her own Oscar someday. But meanwhile, she has a great way to make movies—without even using a camera!

The Oscar award got its nickname from a librarian at the Academy of Motion Pictures. She thought the award statue looked like her uncle Oscar!

Tina

What you're going to make is called a "flip book." It's actually more like a cartoon than a real movie. Each page of the flip book has a still picture on it. Each picture is just a little different from the one before it. When you flip quickly through the pages of the book, it looks as if the still pictures are moving!

Here's how to make your flip book.

Stuff you need:
- black crayon
- ballpoint pen
- a small pad with a glued binding (about 3 × 4 inches)
- scissors

What you do:

1. Carefully cut out the next page. Cut along the dotted lines so that you have four separate pictures.

2. Cover the back of each picture with black crayon.

3. Open your pad to the last page.

4. Line picture #1 up with the bottom and outside edges of the last page. Lay it so the crayon side is down.

5. Use your pen to trace the picture on the paper. Press hard! When you're done, lift picture #1 off the page. There should be crayon lines on the pad where you traced.

6. Turn to the next-to-last page of the pad. Repeat steps 4 and 5 with picture #2.

7. Turn to the third-to-last page of the pad. Repeat steps 4 and 5 with picture #3.

8. Turn to the fourth-to-last page. Repeat steps 4 and 5 with picture #4.

9. Turn to the fifth-to-last page. Now start all over again! Touch up the black crayon coating on the back of picture #1, then repeat steps 4 and 5. And so on!

That's how you start your flip book. Fill the book with drawings from back to front. Once you've finished, flip the pages from front to back. If your drawings are lined up and well traced, it should work!

You can also draw your own pictures for a flip book. I made a flip book about Galaxy Girl. It was way cool—she was flying through space! I did it by drawing her on the bottom of the page and then, page by page, moving her to the top.

Gaby

1

2

3

4

Yo, you've heard about recycling, right? Well, April's the month to get started on it. April is Recycling Month. And April 22 is the big day for the environment—Earth Day.

Recycling means not wasting. There are lots of ways to watch for waste. The Ghostwriter team takes paper, glass, and plastic back to recycling plants where it's reused to make new things. You can also recycle at home. Here's one of the team's ideas!

Are your pockets jammed with pencils, rubber bands, batteries, and other cool stuff you collect during the day? Well, save everything in a "Hold Everything Thing"! You're going to recycle a jar to do this, so get ready.

Stuff you need:
- clean, empty jar
- scissors
- old magazines or newspapers
- glue

What you do:

1. Choose and cut eyes, nose, and mouth from the next page. (Want a different nose or eyes? Go ahead and make your own!)

2. Arrange and glue these pieces to give your jar a face.

3. Cut old newspaper or magazine pages into long strips. Pull the strips along the inner blade of a scissor so that they curl (get a grown-up to help you with this part, so you don't cut yourself).

4. Glue the strips onto the jar to give your Hold Everything Thing hair.

5. Leave the bottom of the jar uncovered so that you can still look in and see what's there.

6. Cut out and glue on letters for your name.

7. Make up a great recycling joke, or a slogan, and write it in the speech bubble on the cut-out page. Cut out the speech bubble and glue it to your Thing's mouth.

I made a Hold Everything Thing for my <u>abuela</u> (that means grandmother) in El Salvador. She says every time she looks at its goofy face, she thinks of me. Hmmm!

Gaby

Here's another Earth Day idea. Tina came up with it after she saw the piles of cards Alex had saved from all his pen pals. Here it is: Get your friends to save all the greeting cards that they receive over the next few months. Then get together and have a happy pad day!

Stuff you need:
- stapler
- old greeting cards
- colored pens, pencils, or markers

What you do:

1. The left (inside) page of a greeting card is usually blank. To make the pads, just tear or cut the cards in half.

2. Staple them together, blank sides up.

3. When you buy a pad of recycled paper at the store, it often has a stamp or logo that says: 100% recycled paper. Design and draw your own logo for the cover of your card-pad! Then staple it on.

THE JOKE'S ON...THE FRIDGE?

April Fools' Day is one day that Ghostwriter's been waiting for all year. He loves jokes! Lenni helped him start a joke collection so that he can leave mysterious joke messages for all his friends on the team.

Want to leave jokes like Ghostwriter does? Get out your favorite jokes and riddles. Write them into the bubbles on the next page. Ask friends, neighbors, and relatives for their best jokes, too.

When you've written out all your jokes, cut out the speech bubbles. Tape them up around your home or school for April Fools' Day. Make sure to put them in funny places. How about inside a kitchen cabinet? On the bathroom mirror? Inside your best friend's notebook?

My mom used to tell lots of knock-knock jokes. They're so corny you can practically hear them popping, but I love them anyway. What's your favorite kind of joke?

Lenni

May is National Physical Fitness month, so on your marks, get set, *go* for Alex's favorite relay races!

Relays are races run in teams. The first runner races from the start to the finish line and back again. Then he or she passes something (say, a stick) to the next runner on the team. That's called the *hand-off*. The next runner runs from start to finish and back. And so on, until everyone on the team has run. The team that finishes first wins. Get it? Got it? Good. Now for the fun part!

Running isn't the only way to get to the finish line. Once Tina was in a race where everyone had to do cartwheels to move forward! There are a zillion weird ways to get where you want to go. Check this one out!

Stuff you need:
- pen or pencil
- scissors

What you do:

1. On page 27, write out your own Goofy Human Tricks. Cut them out along the dotted lines. Alex put in a few of his own favorite ideas to get you started.

2. Trade papers with another team. If you get one that says you have to run while bouncing a ball, then everyone on your team must run the race while bouncing a ball!

3. Start the relay. Each runner on your team must do the Goofy Human Trick when it's their turn to run. The first team to finish wins. Ready, set . . . GO!

Jamal came up with this relay: He got together a bunch of old clothes. Each team got a bag. Each runner had to put on everything in their bag, run to the next person on their team, and take off everything they'd just put on. Gaby looked so funny in Mr. Jenkins's overalls!

Tina

GOOFY HUMAN TRICKS

Run backwards with your right hand on your head.

Run sideways, holding your left ankle.

Skip three times, then twirl like a tornado twice.

PSST!

The sixth sheik's sixth sheep's sick.

Twirling Tina twists thread twice.

Lenni lifts left limbs lightly.

GOOFY HUMAN TRICKS

GOOFY
HUMAN
TRICKS

GOOFY
HUMAN
TRICKS

GOOFY
HUMAN
TRICKS

GOOFY
HUMAN
TRICKS

GOOFY
HUMAN
TRICKS

GOOFY
HUMAN
TRICKS

PSST!

PSST!

PSST!

PSST!

PSST!

PSST!

PSST!

PSST!

By the time you've gone through our Fitness Month relay ideas, you'll be ready for the Olympics! Here's another one. It combines running with an old game called "Whisper Down the Lane." Since it involves talking, naturally it's Gaby's favorite. She dug up some great old tongue twisters. She also made up some new ones about her friends. You can use Gaby's tongue twisters, or you can make up your own.

Stuff you need:
- pen or pencil
- scissors

What you do:

1. Use page 27 to write down a silly sentence. Or you can use one of Gaby's. Cut out your silly sentences along the dotted lines.

2. Trade sentences with another team.

3. Start your relay. But this time, instead of handing off a stick, the first runner will whisper a silly sentence to the next runner, and so on, and so on . . .

4. The last racers to finish have to call out their silly sentences. To win, a team must run the fastest *and* get the silly sentence right!

CATCH YOUR DREAMS!

May may be National Physical Fitness month, but it also happens to be Better Sleep Month. Pretty funny combination, huh? Rob thought up a way to combine sleeping and fitness—it's kind of a workout for your brain.

Here's what you do: Every time you wake up and remember your dream, write down what happened. Use page 31 in this book to record your dreams. Make sure you include the date of each dream. That way you can look back on that date a month from now and know what dream you had!

I read a book about dreaming. It says that everybody dreams, every night. But most of the time, you don't remember your dreams by the time you wake up. Too bad—just think what a neat video game you could make with some of the weird stuff you dream about!

Jamal

I write down all my dreams. I've used some of them in the stories I write. Dreams can come in handy when you're trying to do something creative.

Rob

Dreams from   /   /   **to**   /   /

Date	*Dream*

IT'S ALL RELATIVE

Mother's Day is the second Sunday in May, and the team has a cool way to do something for your mom. And while you do it, you'll find out what she was really like as a kid! Gaby and Alex made up an interview to find out about their mom. You can ask your mother the same questions. Then get the *real* story—ask a relative who knows!

Stuff you need:
- mom
- a relative (like an aunt, uncle, or grandparent) who knew your mom when she was your age
- colored pencils or markers

What you do:

1. Interview your mom. Gaby and Alex's questions will get you started, but you should also ask questions that *you* thought up. What have you always wanted to know? Write down your mom's answers on the interview pages.

2. When you're done interviewing your mom, interview a relative about what your mom was *really* like. Write down the relative's answers under your mom's answers.

3. If you have more questions, make extra interview pages!

4. Share your interview with your mom. If you want, you can cut the interview pages out of this book, decorate them with crayons or markers, and make them into a book.

Interview Questions

1. What did you do for fun? Did you have a favorite sport or hobby?

mom:

relative:

2. What did you want most when you were my age?

mom:

relative:

3. Was there anything you were afraid of?

mom:

relative:

4. Did you like school? What was your favorite subject?

mom:

relative:

5. What did you want to be when you grew up?

mom:

relative:

6. What was your favorite book? Movie? Who was your favorite actor or singer?

mom:

relative:

7. What was the one thing you did that got you in the most trouble when you were my age?

mom:

relative:

8. What were you <u>really</u> like as a kid?

mom:

relative:

GO FLY A KITE!

On June 15, 1752, Ben Franklin conducted a famous experiment that proved lightning is electrical. He went out in a thunderstorm and flew a kite with a key attached to it by a wire. When lightning hit the kite, an electric spark ran down the wire and came out of the key.

Jamal thinks Ben Franklin was cool—so he made his own kite in honor of Franklin's experiment. (Jamal's mom wouldn't let him fly it in a thunderstorm, of course!) You can make your own kite and fly it, too—just don't try the electricity experiment!

Stuff you need:
- a heavy-duty plastic garbage bag
- a felt-tip marker
- a ruler
- scissors
- 6 plastic drinking straws
- tape
- a roll of string

What you do:

1. Cut open the garbage bag and lay it out on the floor.

2. With a felt-tip marker, draw the kite pattern on the bag, as in the drawing on the next page.

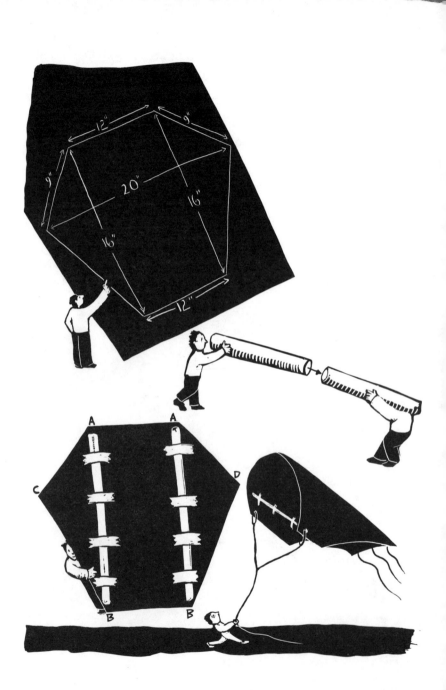

3. Cut out the pattern.

4. Connect three straws by pushing them together at the ends until you have a rod that is 16 inches long. Do this with the other three straws, too.

5. Tape the straws from A to B, as shown in the picture.

6. Punch a small hole at C, and another at D, as shown in the picture.

7. Cut a piece of string 40 inches long. Tie one end of the string through hole C and one through hole D. This is called a bridle.

8. Attach one end of your roll of string to the middle of the bridle. Make sure you have a lot of string to get your kite way up in the sky!

I added a crepe paper tail. It helped keep my kite steady in the air.

Jamal

WHAT'S IN A FACE?

For Father's Day, Lenni made Max a picture album that was all about him. She called it "Dad's Best Moments of the Year" and he's still laughing over it.

Make *your* dad a picture album. Here's what to do:

Stuff you need:

- pen or marker
- scissors
- photographs (you can ask relatives for some, too)
- glue
- heavy paper or cardboard
- stapler

What you do:

1. Find photos for the sections below. If you don't have photos, draw pictures.

2. Decide which photo you want to put in each frame. For some, you might want to cut your pictures to fit the frames. (Get permission before you cut up any photos!)

3. Glue the pictures onto the paper.

4. By each picture, write in funny lines or captions.

5. Cut each page out. Cut a piece of heavy paper or cardboard to make a cover for your photo album. Staple the cover and the photo pages together along the left edge. If you need more pages, make them! Draw your own frames.

J put in a picture of my dad while he was still half asleep. Underneath the photo, J wrote: "Duh—what?" He thought it was funny, too!

Lenni

_____

_____

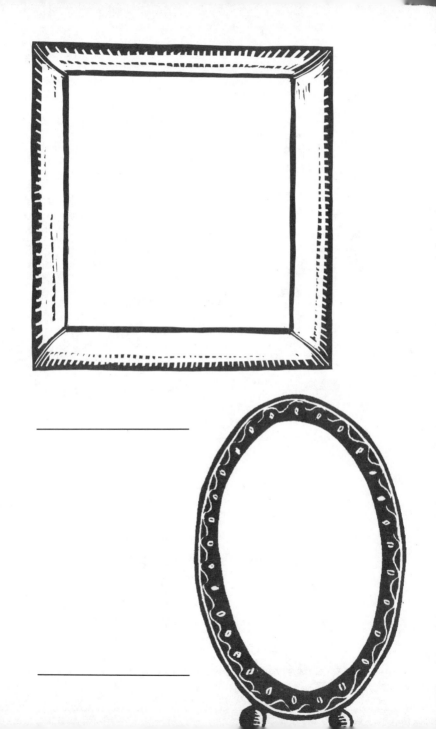

STAMP IT!

Hey, did you know that the U.S. Post Office issued its first stamp way back on July 1, 1847? It's an important date if you're a postal worker, like Jamal's Grandma CeCe.

Some stamps are very valuable. Start saving stamps from envelopes before they get thrown away. Who knows, maybe one day the stamps you collect will be worth a lot of money! Use the next page to start a stamp album. Stick your stamps to the page with a tape loop or a spot of glue. Remember to fill in the year the stamp was printed and, if you include stamps from other countries, what country they came from.

I get cool stamps from all over the world because of my pen pals. If you're a stamp collector, pen pals come in handy!
Alex

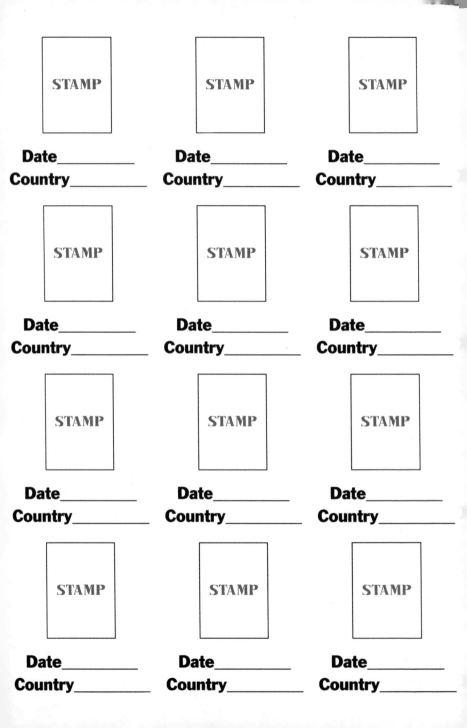

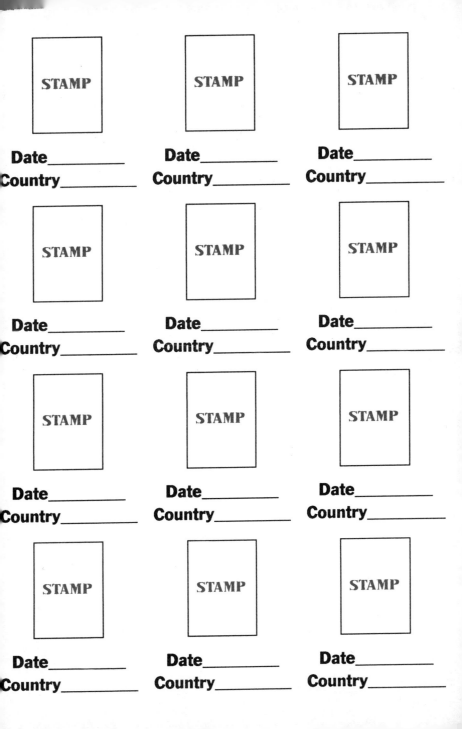

STATE IT!

On the Fourth of July, Independence Day, the team went to the Brooklyn Heights promenade to catch the fireworks. Ghostwriter couldn't see the fireworks, but he had fun checking out all the different license plates on the cars.

Start a collection of all the different license plates you see. Use the pages that follow to write down what each state's plate looks like. What colors are on it? (Write down the color of the numbers *and* the background.) What's the state slogan? Are there any other designs on the plate? Any funny combinations of numbers or letters?

You can also collect license plates from other countries. Some of them look pretty much like U.S. plates, but some are easy to spot because they're a different shape from our plates. Keep a lookout for unusual shapes!

Rob

I saw a great New York license plate that said "Dad's Taxi"!

Gaby

STATE NAME	COLORS ON PLATE	DESIGN	STATE SLOGAN
Alabama			
Alaska			
Arizona			
Arkansas			
California			
Colorado			
Connecticut			
Delaware			
Florida	orange on white	rocket	"Sunshine State"
Georgia			
Hawaii			
Idaho			
Illinois			
Indiana			
Iowa			
Kansas			
Kentucky			

STATE NAME	COLORS ON PLATE	DESIGN	STATE SLOGAN
Louisiana			
Maine			
Maryland			
Massachusetts			
Michigan			
Minnesota			
Mississippi			
Missouri			
Montana			
Nebraska			
Nevada			
New Hampshire			
New Jersey			
New Mexico			
New York	blue on white	Statue of Liberty	"Empire State"
North Carolina			
North Dakota			

STATE NAME	COLORS ON PLATE	DESIGN	STATE SLOGAN
Ohio			
Oklahoma			
Oregon			
Pennsylvania			
Rhode Island			
South Carolina			
South Dakota			
Tennessee			
Texas			
Utah			
Vermont			
Virginia			
Washington			
Washington , D.C.*			
West Virginia			
Wisconsin			
Wyoming			

*Note: Washington, D.C., is not a state, but it does have its own license plate!

Plates from Other Places

NAME	COLORS ON PLATE	DESIGN	SLOGAN

TIME IN A BOX

On August 20, 1977, a probe called *Voyager 2* set out on a long journey through outer space. It's still going today! Besides scientific instruments, *Voyager 2* carries a time capsule containing information about Earth and its people. So if there's anyone out there in space, and they find *Voyager 2*, they'll learn about us!

But a time capsule doesn't have to be for space aliens. You can make one for people right here on Earth. When Rob read about *Voyager 2*, he decided to make his own time capsule. He put in souvenirs from all the different places he's lived, a photo of the Ghostwriter team, a tape of his favorite music, and one of his poems. Then he wrote a letter to the future. In the letter he talked about all the things he hoped would be better in the future and all the things that he liked about the present.

Make your own time capsule. It's easy! Here's how:

Stuff you need:
- a large coffee can
- tape
- marker or pen
- stuff to store
  - — photographs of your friends and family
  - — cards and letters that mean something to you
  - — a list of your favorite music, TV shows
  - — souvenirs from your favorite places
  - — a letter to the future
  - — whatever else you want!

What you do:

1. Put all the stuff to store into the coffee can. Put the lid on the can and seal it with tape.

2. Fill out the next page. Write in your name, the date you made the time capsule, and the date the time capsule may be opened. (Pick a date that you can remember easily, like your birthday.) When you're done, sign your name to make it an official contract.

3. Tape the contract to the can.

4. Store the can in a closet, basement, or attic. Or take it outside and bury it!

5. If you want, open the capsule on the date you wrote in your contract. Check out what's inside—see how much you've changed since you made it. It could be a real blast from the past!

I filled a big jar with stuff that reminds me of my neighborhood, Fort Greene. Then I buried it...but I'm not saying where! Maybe some day in the future someone will dig it up and learn about Brooklyn way back in the 1990s.

Lenni

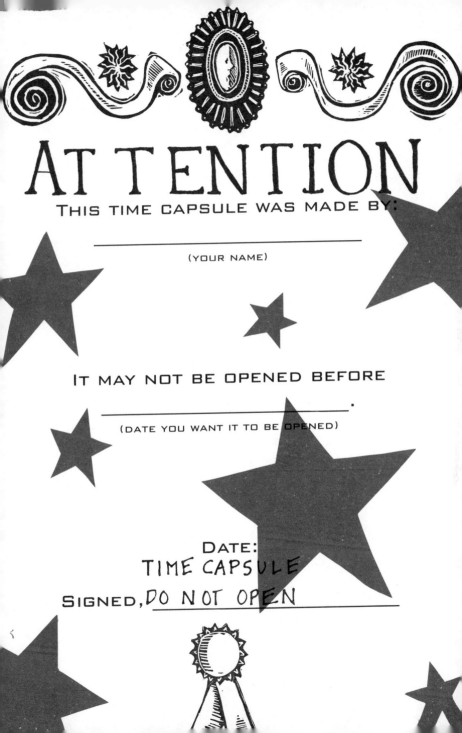

ATTENTION

THIS TIME CAPSULE WAS MADE BY:

_____

(YOUR NAME)

IT MAY NOT BE OPENED BEFORE

_____.

(DATE YOU WANT IT TO BE OPENED)

DATE:

TIME CAPSULE

SIGNED, DO NOT OPEN

YOUR FAMILY TREE

Everyone knows about Labor Day. It's the first Monday in September. Time to go back to school! But what you might not know is that the first Sunday *after* Labor Day is National Grandparents' Day. The Ghostwriter team thinks Grandparents' Day is a much cooler holiday than Labor Day. So do what Jamal did for Grandma CeCe—make a family tree!

I glued real leaves all over my family tree. Grandma CeCe loved that touch!
Jamal

This family tree is easy. All you have to do is write names in the leaf-shaped boxes. Here's what you put in each box:

Box 1: Your name, and the names of all your brothers, sisters, stepbrothers, and stepsisters

Box 2: Parents and stepparents

Box 3: Aunts and uncles (your mother's sisters and brothers)

Box 4: Aunts and uncles (your father's sisters and brothers)

Box 5: First cousins on your mother's side

Box 6: First cousins on your father's side

Box 7: Grandparents on your mother's side

Box 8: Grandparents on your father's side

Box 9: Great-grandparents on your mother's side

Box 10: Great-grandparents on your father's side

Box 11: Great-aunts and -uncles (your mother's aunts and uncles)

Box 12: Great-aunts and -uncles (your father's aunts and uncles)

Now decorate your family tree. You can draw designs on it, or cut out paper leaves to glue down. Or glue on real leaves, like Jamal did. Just make sure they're dried. You can do this by pressing them flat between the pages of a book for a couple of days.

If you want to make your family tree bigger, it's easy. All you have to do is find out more about your family! Who were your grandparents' cousins, aunts, and uncles? Who were your grandparents' grandparents? Make the tree as big as you want!

TURTLE POWER

GabNews Flash: On September 6, 1776, a turtle attacked the British ship *Eagle* in New York Harbor.

Say *what*?

Well, the turtle Gaby's talking about wasn't a cute little reptile. It was one of the first submarines! It was named *Turtle* because, just like a real turtle, it could stay hidden under water and stick its "head"—its periscope—out to scope out the scene.

When Gaby read about the *Turtle*, she had a seriously fun idea. She made her own periscope! Now, like the crew of the *Turtle*, she can see without being seen. Which is handy when you have an older brother to spy on . . .

Now that I have a periscope, I know everything Alex is up to. Ha! He'd be so mad if he found out!

Gaby

Gaby—I found out. And <u>you'd</u> better <u>watch</u> out!

Alex

Here's how to make your own periscope.

Stuff you need:
- a cardboard cookie or cracker box
- 2 small mirrors of the same size
- scissors
- masking tape

What you do:

1. Cut a square hole about one inch by one inch in one side of the box an inch from the top, and another on the opposite side an inch from the bottom. The bottom one is your eye hole.

2. Place the mirrors on an angle at either end of the box, as you see in the picture. The mirror sides should face each other. Look at the drawing to see how it works. It's very important to get the angle of the mirrors just right. Otherwise you won't be able to see anything! So experiment a little— look through the eye hole and move the mirrors around until you get a clear picture.

3. When you have the angle right, tape the mirrors to the sides of the box to hold them in place.

4. Use tape to seal your box at both ends, and your spy periscope is ready to go!

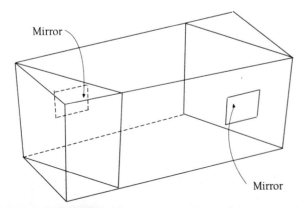

Mirror

Mirror

October 31 . . . It's Halloween, and how does Tina spell fun? G-H-O-S-T! GHOST is a word game you can play anytime, anywhere. All you need are a few friends!

The funny thing about GHOST is that the object of the game is *not* to spell a word. Here's what you do:

1. The first player picks a letter and says it out loud. The second player adds a letter to the first. The next player adds another letter, and so on. Remember, the idea is *not* to spell a word—but here's the catch: You *must* have a word in mind. For example, if the letters already out are W, H, and E, and you add the letter R, then you probably have the word WHERE in mind.

2. Only words of 4 letters or more count as a word in GHOST.

3. The first person to spell a word loses that round and is given a G. He or she is now on the way to collecting the letters that spell GHOST. Once a person has lost five times (G-H-O-S-T), he or she is a ghost and is out of the game.

4. Players can be *challenged* after adding a letter. If the challenged player has bluffed and doesn't have a word in mind, he or she collects a letter and the round is over.

5. Players are not allowed to talk to someone who has become a ghost. They collect a letter each time they do. Ghosts, however, may tell jokes, make funny faces, and do anything they can think of to try to make the players talk or laugh.

6. The last person remaining in the game after all the others have become ghosts is the winner.

7. Use the scorecards on the next page to keep score. (When you run out, make your own scorecards.) In the "Player" column, write down each player's name. Every time a player gets a letter, write down that letter next to his or her name. Whoever wins the most out of 5 rounds is the ultimate GHOST winner!

I LIKE THIS GAME VERY MUCH . . . BUT IT'S HARD TO WIN WHEN YOU'RE A GHOST TO BEGIN WITH!

Player	Letter	Letter	Letter	Letter	Letter

Player	Letter	Letter	Letter	Letter	Letter

CHOW TIME

November is Sandwich Month. Mmmm! Are you ready to whip up one of Lenni's crazy but tasty sandwiches? When you've tried it out, write out your own recipe on the card on the next page! (It has two sides, so you can write down two recipes if you can't decide on one favorite.)

Stuff you need:
- 2 slices of bread
- peanut butter
- chocolate syrup
- ½ banana, sliced
- mini-marshmallows
- raisins

What you do:
1. Spread the peanut butter on one slice of bread.
2. Pour some chocolate syrup over the peanut butter.
3. Place the banana slices over everything.
4. Sprinkle with raisins and mini-marshmallows.
5. Cover with the other slice of bread. Ta-da!

The sandwich was invented over 200 years ago by the Earl of Sandwich. The Earl liked to play cards so much that he didn't want to stop—even to eat! So he ordered his food brought to him between slices of bread. That way he could hold his dinner in one hand and his cards in the other!

Gaby

Sandwiches are fine, but personally, I'm more into pizza. And guess what? October is Pizza Month! Jam on it!

Alex

_____'s Seriously Slammin' Sandwich

Stuff you need:

What you do:

_____'s Seriously Slammin' Sandwich

Stuff you need:

What you do:

On December 14, bird-watchers all over the country begin to count the different kinds of birds that spend winters near them. This year, Rob plans to do it, too. He's betting that there are more birds in Brooklyn than most people think!

To help prove his point, Rob needs to attract some birds. So he made this simple bird feeder to hang outside his window. You can make one, too. It's easy—here's how!

Stuff you need:
- small chunk of wood or large pinecone
- piece of string (about 36 inches)
- peanut butter
- flour or cornmeal
- birdseed

What you do:

1. Tie one end of the string around your chunk of wood.

2. Put several large spoonfuls of peanut butter in a bowl. Mix with a little flour or cornmeal, until the oil in the peanut butter is soaked up. (Oil is bad because if it gets on a bird's feathers, they get all glopped up and the bird can't keep warm anymore.)

3. Spread the peanut butter and flour mixture over the piece of wood until it's coated.

4. Sprinkle birdseed on the piece of wood. It will stick to the peanut butter mixture.

5. Tie your bird feeder outside your window! If there's a tree branch near your window, tie it to that. If you don't have a tree near your window, find something else. How about a window box?

6. When the birdseed is all gone, make sure to put more out on your feeder. Birds have a hard time finding food in the winter—the ones that eat from your feeder will learn to depend on it!

Birds have to eat all the time. Some days they eat enough food to equal 4/5 of their body weight. Think what that would mean for you. If you weigh 60 pounds, you would have to eat 48 pounds of food in one day—that's about 190 hamburgers!

Rob

Now that you have your feeder, use Rob's chart to keep track of all the different kinds of birds that visit it.

IF YOU WANT TO KNOW MORE ABOUT THE BIRDS YOU SEE, TAKE A TRIP TO YOUR LOCAL LIBRARY. THEY'VE GOT BOOKS THAT WILL TELL YOU WHATEVER YOU WANT TO KNOW.

Bird Watch

Date	Description of Bird

Bird Watch

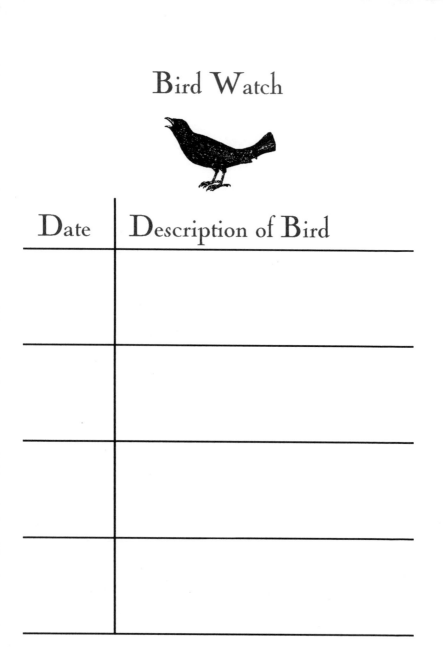

Date	Description of Bird

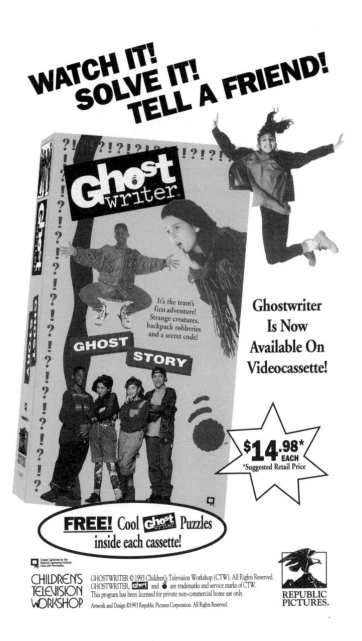

BECOME AN OFFICIAL
GHOSTWRITER READERS CLUB MEMBER!

You'll receive the following GHOSTWRITER Readers Club Materials:
Official Membership Card • The Scoop on GHOSTWRITER •
GHOSTWRITER Magazine
All members registered by December 31st will have a chance to win
a FREE COMPUTER and other exciting prizes!

O F F I C I A L   E N T R Y   F O R M

Mail your completed entry to: Bantam Doubleday Dell BFYR,
GW Club, 1540 Broadway, New York, NY 10036

Name

Address

City   **State**   **Zip**

Age   **Phone**

Club Sweepstakes Official Rules
1. No purchase necessary. Enter by completing and returning the Entry Coupon. All entries must be received by Bantam
   Doubleday Dell no later than December 31, 1993. No mechanically reproduced entries allowed. By entering the
   sweepstakes, each entrant agrees to be bound by these rules and the decision of the judges which shall be final and binding.
   Limit: one entry per person.
2. The prizes are as follows: Grand Prize: One computer with monitor (approximate retail value of Grand Prize $3,000), First
   Prizes: Ten GHOSTWRITER libraries (approximate retail value of each First Prize: $25), Second Prizes: Five GHOSTWRITER
   backpacks (approximate retail value of each Second Prize: $25), and Third Prizes: Ten GHOSTWRITER T-Shirts (approximate
   retail value of each Third Prize: $10). Winners will be chosen in a random drawing on or about January 10, 1994, from
   among all completed Entry Coupons received and will be notified by mail. Odds of winning depend on the number of
   entries received. No substitution or transfer of the prize is allowed. All entries become property of BDD and will not be
   returned. Taxes, if any, are the sole responsibility of the winner. BDD reserves the right to substitute a prize of equal or
   greater value if any prize becomes unavailable.
3. This sweepstakes is open only to the residents of the U.S. and Canada, excluding the Province of Quebec, who are between
   the ages of 6 and 14 at the time of entry. The winner, if Canadian, will be required to answer correctly a time-limited
   arithmetical skill testing question in order to receive the prize. Employees of Bantam Doubleday Dell Publishing Group Inc.
   and its subsidiaries and affiliates and their immediate family members are not eligible. Void where prohibited or restricted
   by law. Grand and first prize winners will be required to execute and return within 14 days of notification an affidavit of
   eligibility and release to be signed by winner and winner's parent or legal guardian. In the event of noncompliance with
   this time period, an alternate winner will be chosen.
4. Entering the sweepstakes constitutes permission for use of the winner's name, likeness, and biographical data for publicity
   and promotional purposes on behalf of BDD, with no additional compensation. For the name of the winner, available after
   January 31, 1994, send a self-addressed envelope, entirely separate from your entry, to Bantam Doubleday Dell, BFYR
   Marketing Department, 1540 Broadway, New York, NY 10036.